IT'S NOT AS SIMPLE AS THAT

Jules Vienna

STEEMROK

Steemrok Publishing
Chesham, England

steemrok.com

Author's Note

All of the characters and events in this book are fictitious apart from the obvious exceptions such as the September 11 atrocities and the hurricane which devasted New Orleans.

Of the three railway accidents mentioned in Chapter 7 the two fatal crashes were real occurrences, at Quintinshill near Gretna Green in 1915 and at Harrow in 1952 respectively. The Aylesbury accident is fictitious. For artistic purposes the working pattern and regulatory regime for train drivers described in this book are based on aviation practices and therefore may differ in reality from those in the railway industry. The Public Transport Inspectorate is fictional. There is, sadly, no overall body responsible for public transport safety in this country. Responsibility is split between several agencies, including the Health and Safety Executive. By contrast, in the United States the National Transportation Safety Board oversees all public transport enterprises.

CHAPTER 1

It's not easy being 12 years old. When you're a kid, like my 6 year old sister Amy, you don't understand lots of things. But by the time you get to my age you know what's what. Except that old people still talk to you like you still don't understand. For example, the teacher told us that the world's population is going up by 80 million people every year. Eighty million! Every year! That sounds scary to me. I mean, that's like more than all the people that can fit in a thousand football stadiums! Every year! I said it was scary but the teacher shook her head. No, she said, the rate of increase is slowing down so 80 million is a good number. It used to be worse, she said.

Okay, so where's all the food coming from to feed all these extra people? Also, where are they going to put all the rubbish they produce - cornflake packets and computer game boxes and stuff like that. Also, if they go to the toilet every day where will all the extra shit go? I didn't say that last bit to the teacher, of course. It's okay for adults to swear - they do it all the time - but we get bollocked if they hear us do it. Anyway, I was expecting the usual answer. It's always the same. You tell them something obvious that even a 5 year old can understand and they go 'It's not as simple as that'. In other words 'I know you're right but I'm not allowed to say so'. But amazingly the teacher said I had a good point! Course I got a lot of stick from my mates afterwards - now I'm a teacher's pet and I'll have to do something bad to cancel it out.

The only old person who says stuff I can understand is my friend Justin's auntie. Considering she's so old – she's nearly 30 – it's amazing how smart she is. Her name's Charlotte but everyone calls her Charlie. (Justin calls her Charlotte the Harlot.) Justin's Dad is always taking the piss out of her - calls her a commie or a pinko. You probably know that commie means communist, which means someone who's jealous of rich people. Pinko is something to do with politics. It could be skin colour - my Dad says pinkos love black people. But that's weird - okay, Charlie has got pink skin but so have I and my Mum and my sisters and none of us are bothered one way or the other about black people. Ollie - he's one of my best mates at school - he's black. She looks nice and smells nice, Charlie, and her boyfriend always buys us crisps and stuff. He's brilliant, Martin. He drives express trains weighing hundreds of tons and carrying hundreds of people. Justin's Dad doesn't like him because he and Charlie gang up on him when they're having arguments. Martin goes to rock concerts. He's going to take me one day when I'm older if my Dad will let me. My Dad's as useless as Justin's Dad. He's an estate agent, selling crappy houses to gullible punters, to use his own words. Gullible is nothing to do with gulls, by the way. I don't know what it means but it's obviously something not good. If it wasn't for the fact that my Dad supports Tottenham he'd be a complete plonker.

My Mum's sort of okay, but she's a bit of a wally. She's a teacher but not at my school, thank God. I know she's smarter than Dad but she never argues with him even when he's talking bollocks. She's also dead old fashioned. She made me learn my tables when no-one else in my class had to and she tells me off when I spell words wrong. Now that is stupid. Why can't you spell words like they sound? Supposing you were a foreign person trying to learn English. How the hell are you supposed to work out that 'cough' sounds like 'coff'? Why isn't 'English' spelt 'Inglish'? Charlie says there should be two Englishes. One sort of proper English for reading the news on telly with a proper accent or writing books with proper spelling and then like talking English when you can say what you like whatever way you want to say it. What were those words she said - 'collo cweel' or something. Usually I agree with Charlie but she's wrong on this one. Why do you need proper English - it's obvious you can use collo cweel English for everything.

I'm not brilliant at school work, not like my sister Alice who is dead clever. She passed her 11 plus easily and goes to the Girls' Grammar. She is so naff, my sister, it's untrue. She does her homework without being told to and she keeps her room tidy. It's so embarrassing when my friends come round. Once I messed up her room just to make it look more normal but wow, did I get into trouble. I told them Amy (my little sister) did it but no-one believed me. I admit I felt bad about trying to blame Amy, the daft little cow. As punishment, my Mum banned me from going to White Hart Lane that Saturday, so I missed seeing West Ham get stuffed 3-1.

I didn't pass the 11 plus – not properly anyway. But my Mum went to see someone she knew in the Education Department and told them I should have passed. So instead of going to the Senior School where I would've had an cushy time I have to go to the Mixed Grammar where they make me learn stuff I don't understand. Charlie says the 11 plus is unfair, because only about one third of the children pass it. So two thirds go to the Senior Schools instead of the Grammars and everyone says the Senior Schools are crap (except my Mum, who teaches at one of them. In that case why did she want me to go to the MG?) My Dad reckons it's only right that the best children should get the best teaching but he only said it after we found out I'd passed after all.

Charlie says all the schools should be the same but she also says that kids clever at some things should be taught together. Maths and French and stuff like that. Streaming - that's what they call it. Mum says the British don't take education seriously but it seems serious enough to me, the amount of stuff we're supposed to learn, not to mention SATs and bloody homework! I think what Mum means is that teachers should get more pay and I think she's right. Then she wouldn't have to drive around in that tatty little green car. Green, for Christ's sake! She doesn't understand when I don't want to get in it.

Mr Morris, our school headmaster, is a complete turd. The creepiest creep in the whole wide world. He's all smarmy when he talks to parents or when he's giving speeches. He talks dead posh but he's useless at running the school. He's also a snob. My Mum was talking to him once when another mother came over, who happened to be the wife of the Mayor. Morris cut Mum dead and started smarming up to the Mayor's wife. What an arsehole! I saw it with my own eyes. When I told the other kids they said we should get him back so Timbo pissed on the seat of his car. Brilliant!

Actually, despite Morris the Turd I don't mind school. Most of the teachers are okay, especially the ones who don't like the headmaster. Morris once gave me a detention for talking in assembly when it wasn't me who did it. Obviously I couldn't grass up the real culprit, Ollie, who was already in trouble. I'm not bad at art and music but I'm crap at maths, even though I know my tables. At least the MG isn't as bad as Orchard Academy, where the thick children of rich parents go. Everyone says it's full of gays and nutters.

The best teacher at my school is Bob Hollis. We get him for history and geography. He tells us amazing stuff. He got told off by Mrs Bellwood for teaching us that Jesus Christ was just a political activist like John Lennon, who used to be a rock singer until he got shot. Mrs Bellwood does RE. Her opinion is that Jesus was the son of God but let's face it - where's the evidence? Why wasn't his mother a God too? According to the New Bible we have to read the Christs were a poor family - Jesus was born in a stable with a load of animals. Not very cool for the son of God. These miracles he did - pretty simple stuff, changing water into wine, feeding loads of people with a few fish sandwiches. Okay, he is supposed to have brought some bloke back to life but was he really dead in the first place? Was Jesus really dead when he did the same trick on himself?

Is there a God for Jesus to be son of? And who created God? And who created the person who created God? If someone created the universe they made a pretty crap job of it. What's the point of having diseases? Why do people get dozy as they get older? Why can't people get smarter and healthier instead? Why do people have to die anyway? What's the point of earthquakes and droughts and floods? Why are so many grown-ups so miserable or so shitty? It's true, you know. You never get children who are as miserable or as shitty as grown-ups. Mrs Bellwood gets annoyed when you say this stuff. She says you have to have faith in God. Doesn't seem like much of a deal to me. The best way for God to make you believe in him would be to beam down to earth in the middle of the World Cup final. You couldn't argue with that.

'. . . MR HOLLIS IS A SUBVERSIVE . . . THAT'S LIKE A BOAT THAT CAN GO UNDERWATER, LIKE A SMALL SUBMARINE . . . '

Charlie doesn't believe in God. She says why do people use the Bible to tell us what to do when it was written 2000 years ago by people who thought the earth was flat and floods were God's punishment for being bad. But Martin says some people need God to help them when they're unhappy and it's wrong to tell these people that God doesn't exist.

Charlie reckons religion is a con trick. You tell people to put up with being poor or having a shitty life because when you die you go straight to heaven and live happily ever after. She says that religion is used as political control but I don't really know what that means. She laughed when I told her what Bob Hollis said about more people have been killed in the name of God than any other reason. My Dad says Mr Hollis is a subversive. I think that's like a boat that can go under water like a small submarine. I can't see the connection myself.

There's one thing I like about religion and that's the music although of course I wouldn't dare admit it to my friends. They already take the piss because I do piano lessons with Miss Hochdorfer who's an old foreign woman. If there's no-one at home I watch services on the telly. Some of the hymns have terrific tunes, even if the words are stupid. Don't laugh, but I've even made up some hymn tunes myself. I play them on my sister's Yamaha which can store stuff in its memory. I even tried to think of words in church-type English. One went:

Jesus thou art son of God
Upon this impious world thou trod
Thou fed the throng with crumbs of bread
Pray guard my soul when I be dead

I don't know what 'impious' means or even how you're supposed to say it but it looks good. On the radio on Wednesday afternoons they have choral evensong from one of the big cathedrals. The music is brilliant. One minute you get chanting - plainsong I think it's called, then you get these brill anthems with full harmony. Last Easter the junior classes went to hear the St Matthew Passion at St Paul's Cathedral. It was fantastic although of course I had to pretend it was boring like the other kids. I even did a mega fart to make the others laugh but I did it in one of the quiet bits rather than a chorus. (They wouldn't have heard it if I'd done it in a chorus anyway.)

My Dad says he's a Christian but he never goes to church. He says he doesn't go because only coloured people and social misfits and snobs go to church. So, I said, what about all people being equal in the eyes of God, which is what Mrs Bellwood told us. Also, why do they send out loads of planes and helicopters out when someone falls off a boat in the Channel but no-one seems to be bothered when thousands of Bangladesh people get drowned in floods. Guess what Dad said. The usual answer. 'It's not as simple as that'.

CHAPTER 2

Martin's going to get me a ride on one of his trains. He's got to get special permission for me to go in the front with him. He drives these big fast electric trains that do 125 miles per hour. He's nuts about trains. He drives steam engines in his spare time on the Sussex Steam Line near Brighton. He's taken me a couple of times. These old engines are a bit scary. They hiss like they're about to explode and they smell disgusting, like burning wet wood. But they look amazing - massive wheels joined by like girders that clank when the wheels go round and steam leaking out from the pipes. And there's a huge furnace in the cab where they have to shovel coal into to make the steam. When they open the fire door you can see the coal glowing red hot and you can feel the heat.

According to Martin some of the steam engines could go nearly as fast as the trains he drives, which is amazing. Why don't modern trains go faster? He says they do, but not in Britain. Other countries have faster trains but for some reason we can't have them here. When I asked him why not he gave me some complicated answer about politics which I can't remember apart from the bit about foreign countries spending more money on trains and stuff like that. As soon as someone says 'politics' I know I won't understand what they're talking about.

Martin says people should use trains more but you can't get to the shops in a train, can you? Anyway he drives his car to work himself. But it's obvious there are too many cars around. You see the adverts on the telly where these shiny new cars whizz around on roads with no other traffic. Of course in real life most of the roads are jam packed with cars and trucks crawling along with smoke belching out from their exhaust pipes. I told Martin that traffic fumes don't smell as bad as steam engines but he didn't agree. They don't bother me unless we're stuck in a jam for a long time. Then I sometimes get a headache and my windpipe feels funny, like something's stuck in it. What I don't understand is - why does everyone go to work at the same time? Even my stupid sister Amy could work out that if there are too many cars and everyone drives to work at the same time you're going to get traffic jams.

It's like school - all the kids go to school at the same time and go home at the same time so all the school buses and all the mums taking their kids in the car are all getting in each other's way. Why not start some days later for some of the kids, which also means you could stay longer in bed instead of going to school half asleep and trying to stay awake when the teacher's going on about something boring.

I had a brilliant idea once. You know how buses wait at the bus stops for ages because the driver has to collect ticket money - why not get another person to do the tickets? Then, instead of blocking the road for years the driver could drive off as soon as the passengers were on board and then the ticket person could collect the fare money while the bus was moving. When I told Martin, guess what? He said that in some places they actually do that. I was dead chuffed that one of my ideas was so good that someone else had copied it, even though it proved that they had thought of it first. So why don't they do it on all buses? You can guess what the answer would be if I asked a grown-up.

I was telling you about Mr Hollis a while ago. He also takes us for science. Sometimes it's interesting and sometimes it's boring. We did the solar system the other day. Did you know the moon goes round the world at nearly 4000 kilometres per hour? And yet when you look at it you can't see it moving, because it's so far away, like about 400,000 kilometres or something. But that's nothing - the sun is 150 *million* kilometres away. That's so far away that it takes light rays eight minutes to get from the sun to the earth. So if the sun went out you'd still see it shining for another eight minutes. But get this - the sun makes all its heat and light from nuclear energy, like an everlasting nuclear bomb. Mr Hollis said it does it by destroying itself. It actually destroys its own matter by changing hydrogen into helium. And do you know how much? I'll tell you - it destroys 4 billion kilograms of itself every second. That's right - *four billion!* Timbo asked him how long the sun was going to last. Mr Hollis laughed. He said there's several million years of hydrogen left yet. I hope he's right!

Mr Hollis was doing the lesson on Powerpoint. But then he picked up a marker and drew a picture on the board – the sun, the moon and the earth in a straight line. Then he drew a line from the top of the sun, touching the top of the moon to a spot on the earth. Then he drew another line from the bottom of the sun, touching the bottom of the moon and meeting the same spot on the earth as the first one.

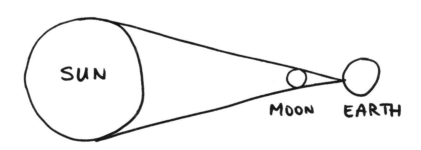

THE DIAGRAM THAT MR HOLLIS DREW

The teacher said that the sun and moon looked the same size when we see them because it just so happens that the distances and sizes matched each other even though the sun was much bigger than the moon and much farther away. Because of this we get amazing eclipses sometimes, when the moon exactly covers the sun and you can see the burning gases round the sun's edge and stars round about, just like the eclipse in 1999. Mr Hollis said it was an amazing coincidence that the sun and moon seemed to be the same size, less than the chance of winning the lottery. So the question is, he asked us, is why this happened to be?

Timbo and I looked at each other and Timbo did his 'who gives a shit' look. Then Sarah – it had to be Sarah – said, 'Are you suggesting that God made the moon the correct size?'

Mr Hollis smiled and said, 'Who knows?' Just as well Mrs Bellwood wasn't there. She would have told him off and said of course it was God who did it.

We go on school outings sometimes. We had a look round a dairy the other week but it wasn't very interesting, although there was this massive machine that looked like a ginormous tumble drier that turned cream into butter. The best bit was some of us were allowed to have a go on the fork lift which takes the boxes of butter into the storage place. Dave Bresson managed to stick one of the prongs into one of the boxes and all this butter splurged out. It was mega, but Mrs Hicks wasn't very amused and neither was the man in charge of the butter machine. Mrs Hicks is one of our teachers. She's a bit of a misery most of the time. She gave Dave a right bollocking and no-one else got a go on the fork lift after that.

Another trip was the British Museum, which was mainly boring. There were some students outside carrying signs about sending back some marbles which belong to Greece. Big deal! Surely the Greeks can get some new marbles of their own - they don't cost much after all. Inside it was mainly old statues and pots and stuff like that. But there was one good thing Mrs Hicks showed us - the Rosetta stone. Some French soldiers found it in Egpyt a long time ago. It's a big black slab completely covered in old writing with some bits missing where the stone was broken. The top bit is picture words - higher graphics they're called. Underneath are letters but they don't look like normal letters. Greek I think Mrs Hicks said. Anyway, some clever geezer worked out what the picture words meant by matching them up to the letter words underneath and that's how they work out what's written in these Egyptian tombs and so on.

I'm quite good at games - football and rugby mainly and cricket just about. I'm sometimes in the first eleven for football for my year, usually as a defender although I can also run fast with the ball except that the games teacher, Mr Sadiq, says that I lose possession too easily although I think I'm not as bad as he makes out. I wouldn't mind being a professional footballer when I grow up but I'm probably not good enough for that. Maybe I could get a job writing church music but I don't know how much money I would get. Also I'd have to make sure that no-one found out because it would be so embarrassing. I'd have to pretend I was doing secret work for the Government or something. If I made it as a footballer I'd probably make more money. I mean, those guys in the Premier League, they make a fortune. If I made

'I'D LIKE TO GET MY HANDS ON
A CHURCH ORGAN'

good money I could do music as a hobby and I could buy a big house and put a real organ in it, not some piddly little Yamaha keyboard.

I'd really like to get my hands on a church organ with three keyboards and pedals too. Not just loud and soft pedals like a piano but proper notes. The only person I've told that I want to play an organ is Miss Hochdorfer, my piano teacher. She wouldn't tell anyone. She's about 200 years old and a bit deaf. I even have to play quiet bits loud so she can hear. But she's alright, Miriam - that's her name. She doesn't mind me playing pop music sometimes. She told me how you get high notes and low notes. You won't believe this but music is really vibrating air. If you make it vibrate slow you get low notes. Fast makes high notes. In a piano the bass strings are thicker so they vibrate slower. In an organ the long pipes do the same thing so they give the bass notes.

Martin was on the telly yesterday, talking about trains. There was a crash not long ago when a train came off the rails. Martin is a sort of spokesman in the drivers' union which is why he was being interviewed. He said that maybe the driver was tired because they have to work harder now. It's like Mum, always going on about teachers having too much work and not enough pay. Not at my school! Any time you go to the staff room half of them are lounging around reading the paper and gassing.

Work's a funny thing. People without jobs get money from the government for doing nothing. Sounds brill to me, though Charlie says they don't get enough. My Dad says they get too much. But what I don't understand is that the people who work say there's too much work for them to do, like Martin and the train drivers. So why not share out the work between all the people, so everyone's got a job and no one has to work too hard. Guess what the answer would be if I asked a grown-up. Actually, Charlie said I had a good point and Martin should put it in his speech. What's happening is Martin is in some sort of election for the drivers' union and he's got to make a speech asking people to vote for him. What about that, eh? My very own idea in a grown-up speech.

It's like why don't rich countries give money to poor countries? Or even food. You'd probably get the usual answer. You see all these starving Africans on the news but at our school half the food gets chucked away. Okay, it usually tastes like vomit but if you were starving you'd eat it, except maybe tapioca pudding. It doesn't seem fair that the Africans have to live in tents with no money and no food while the Queen lives in a huge palace with like servants to do everything for her and millions of pounds to spend on food and clothes.

My Mum and Dad are good friends with Justin's Dad and his Aunt Charlotte but they often start arguing when they come round for a drink specially when they talk about the royal family. Charlie says we should have a president, like America but no one agrees with her. If they asked me - they never do - I would say that having a queen or a king is better because it's like more historical but the people should be allowed to choose who the queen was, maybe Britney Spears. She wouldn't need a palace - just a big house. The money from selling CDs could pay for it. Then you could sell the palace to get money to buy food for the Africans. Or if it was a king you could have some one like David Beckham. Or else you could make Prince Charles the new President if enough people voted for him. Then he wouldn't have to wait till the Queen died. My Dad says if he wins the lottery he's going to give some money to the Government so that he can be a Lord. Then he reckons he'll be able to change the laws to stop immigrants coming to England. That would be really cool – imagine saying to the other kids at school 'you can't touch me, my Dad's a Lord.' Also the teachers wouldn't be able to tell me off.

Justin's Mum went off with another man a couple of years ago. We're not supposed to talk about it. Justin was all moody for a bit but he's a bit better now. Charlie and Martin live in the same house as Justin's Dad. His Dad's got a new girlfriend but she doesn't live in the house with the others. I've met her a couple of times - she's dead posh and walks around with her nose in the air. She's called Penelope or something. She talks funny, like the queen. All the royal family talk like that. Maybe they have special lessons or maybe that's what happens when you go to those special schools they go to. According to Justin royal children aren't allowed to go to normal schools because they aren't very clever and they wouldn't understand the lessons. But she's also cool, Penelope, even though she had a go at me for drawing a picture of the Union flag upside down. When people tell her off for smoking she says they do more damage to the atmosphere with their cars and cheap flights than she does with her ciggies. She goes fox-hunting too, which is against the law. I don't like the idea of foxes being ripped to pieces by dogs – Charlie says it's bullying and sets a bad example to children. But Justin's Dad's got a photo of Penelope in her red hunting outfit sitting on a horse and she looks really great. The flag thing was that the red stripe going across at an angle is not in the middle of the white stripe – it's supposed to be off to one side a bit. So I said to Penelope does it matter? Anyway, why not have the red stripe in the middle, then there wouldn't be a right way up or a wrong way up. Guess what she said: 'It's not as simple as that'!

Sometimes Martin argues with Justin's Dad, usually about music. Martin reckons that it's pop music that stops war. According to Martin, young people all over the world listen to bands like Led Zeppelin and David Bowie. What was it he said? How can you drop bombs on people in China or Iraq who are listening to Metallica or Dead Dogs? My Dad said that was a good reason to bomb them but he was laughing when he said it.

Maybe it's football that stops wars. When England goes to war it's always against Germany but now with the European Cup and the Champions' League and all that stuff it would be impossible to fight them because the football would have to stop. Mr Hollis was telling us about wars still going on in the world. It's interesting that you get like America against Iraq and Israel against the Arabs but if they played football against each other the wars would have to stop.

'NAPOLEON WAS BEATEN BY WELLINGTON WHEN HE GOT OFF THE TRAIN AT WATERLOO'

Actually, in the old days England used to fight France all the time. That proves the theory - they never used to have football then. There was a French Emperor called Napoleon who was good at fighting till he came to England. When he got off the train at Waterloo he got beaten by the English army, led by the Duke of Wellington, who invented the wellie boot. Mr Hollis told us Napoleon lost the Battle of Waterloo because he was unwell. Dave Bresson asked him if it was because he had piles and Mr Hollis laughed. No one knew what Dave was talking about. Piles of what? Mr Hollis made Dave explain it to us - Dave's Mum is a nurse. Dave said piles is another way of saying a pain in the bum. I said in that case Morris the headmaster was piles but I said it quietly so the teacher wouldn't hear. So there you go - don't go fighting battles if your arse is sore.

CHAPTER 3

Yesterday I got a surprise. We were doing Social Studies - boring, boring - when Andy Magillan passed me a note. Andy's a good bloke. When he was a baby he came over from Ireland with his family to get away from the fighting. His Gran was killed by a bomb - she was in a greengrocer's shop when it exploded. Six people were killed, including Andy's Gran. Anyway, what was I telling you about? Oh yeah, the note. It wasn't from Andy himself - it was from Sheila Ashley, who sits in front of Andy, who sits in front of me. Do I want to go out with her, the note said. I was amazed. I like Sheila, she's not as stupid as the other girls and the note said she supports Tottenham. But, let's face it, 'going out with' means having sex, which I haven't done yet.

Of course I know what sex is all about - we get lessons at school and the videos are really funny. But I don't know if I want to do it yet. Does that mean I'm gay? Timbo says he's done it with an older girl but he's probably making it up. The strange thing is my willy goes stiff for no reason, like when I'm on the bus thinking about nothing. Maybe there's something wrong with it, but of course I can't tell anyone. I'm only telling you because you're a stranger and I'll never meet you. It doesn't go stiff when I think about Sheila

Ashley. What should I do? I thought of telling her that I'm already going out with another girl but what would she say? Would she be angry? Maybe I should ask Charlie - she seems to know everything and she wouldn't tell anyone about my problem.

'PARENTS COULD TAKE THE EGG
DOWN THE PUB'

You have to have sex to have children, as you know. Mr Hollis told us about DNA, which is like a molecule that decides what shape you'll be and what colour your hair will be and stuff like that. When your dad shags your mum bits of their DNA join up to make the baby's DNA, which is why you look like your parents. You can see that Alice and Amy are sisters by just looking at them. Luckily I'm not as ugly as they are.

I'm glad I'm not a girl. At least I won't have to have babies when I grow up. Okay, my sisters are ugly, but not as ugly as a woman about to have a baby. It's revolting - they look like hot-air balloons and they walk like ducks on the towpath. Mr Hollis said humans are not as advanced as crocodiles and snakes - they're reptiles and they lay eggs instead. Ollie got a laugh in class when he suggested women should lay eggs. It started a general discussion. I said the eggs could be kept warm by sticking them in the airing cupboard and Timbo reckoned the parents could take the egg down the pub and take turns sitting on it, like birds do in their nests.

Dave Bresson said the reason he was crap at lessons was because his parents had given him the wrong DNA, but Bob Hollis said no, he was just lazy. We all laughed, but the teacher turned dead serious. Consider yourselves lucky you were reasonably bright, he told us. You might have been born stupid, which was just about the worst thing in the world. If you were born stupid nothing could make you clever, even if your parents were rich and sent you to an expensive private school. 'Remember children,' he said, 'money can't buy intelligence.'

So I told the class what Justin said about the children of the Royal Family not being clever enough to go to normal schools. For once Mr Hollis didn't have a funny answer. He didn't say anything for a minute and we all looked at each other, wondering if he'd gone funny. Then he said the Royal Family couldn't choose who they married, so they didn't give themselves the chance of marrying someone clever, so therefore the children couldn't be clever . . . or something like that. The bell went then so that was the end of that.

Mrs Hicks was talking about about marriage in Social Studies. Luckily she didn't talk about sex when Ollie tried to make her. I sniggered like the other boys but really I get embarassed. She told us marriage wasn't as bad as Mr Hollis made out, which puzzled us because he hadn't even mentioned it. She said less than half of them broke up these days, which was pretty good going. Timbo said he saw on the telly that there was a design fault with the human being. When Hicksy asked him what he meant he said the telly said that when a woman loves a man she never fancies anyone else at the same time, but a man fancies other women even if he loves the woman he's attached to. He tried to remember the words - women were monotonous but men were polly something. Hicksy said yes, he was right, but good men stopped themselves fancying other women. Timbo said he'd shag 'em all but not loud enough for the teacher to hear.

Funny though, when you think about Justin's Mum. She was the one who went off with another man, not his Dad going off with another woman. I didn't say this though. All the kids in my class know Justin, even though he's in the other class, but they don't know about his Mum. I don't mind Justin's Dad but he's sort of hard on poor people - says they've only got themselves to blame by not working harder to get more money. Guess what? Charlie told him the normal answer I get - 'it's not as simple as that!'

When they were talking about traffic jams the other day Justin's Dad said cars and petrol should be more expensive so poor people couldn't afford them. What started it was Justin and I were late for school cos a huge artic got stuck trying to go round the mini roundabout nearby. In the end we got out of the bus and walked. Why do they let mega-sized trucks go on little roads? Martin came out with his standard answer - put the stuff on trains - and we all groaned, even Charlie! Martin's got weird ideas about cars and stuff. He reckons they should be fitted with a sort of gadget that stops them going too fast and he says drivers should take a test every 5 years. My Mum would kill him - she had to take her test about 1000 times before she got her licence, so Dad says anyway. Martin also says people should have to take extra tests if they want to go fast or drive big cars. Sounds like he should be a teacher – tests, tests, tests all the time!

Bob Hollis nearly got into trouble the day of the stuck lorry. When we told him why we were late someone in the class said there were too many big cars - you know, the ones that look like army jeeps. They're called off road vehicles or something but you always see them on the road. Hollis said something about it which no-one paid any attention to. Anyway, the next day, I was in Morris the Turd's office to collect next week's Class Mission Statement when this woman came in and started shouting the odds, telling him to give Hollis the elbow. She stuck a bit of paper in Morris's face and said 'I've sent a copy of this to the governors. I want an apology from Mr Hollis and I want him sacked.'

Morris read the paper while this hag was yelling at him. Turned out she was Sarah Haywood's mother. For once Morris did the right thing and tried to calm her down. Said it was probably a misunderstanding and he would have a word with Bob Hollis about it. After Mrs Haywood had gone I sneaked the paper off the desk while The Turd wasn't looking, thinking to myself I bet it's about sex. No such luck. Talk about boring - neither Timbo or Dave Bresson or me could make out what it meant. This is what it said: 'I own a Geronimo Super Scout vehicle. My daughter came home from school today and told me that Mr Hollis had said not all owners of four wheel drive vehicles were compensating for personality inadequacies. This is grossly insulting and Hollis should apologise personally to all owners of these vehicles and should then be dismissed.' What do you make of that? Typical Sarah. She says big words that no-one else understands, but otherwise she's cool. She gets us cigarettes sometimes and she's let Dave touch her tits. I don't think she meant to get Bob Hollis into trouble. More like showing off how clever she is.

On the subject of posh cars, we were talking about poverty in Social Studies. Hicksy got all serious and asked us if rich people had a duty to help poor people. I mean - who bloody knows? She should be telling us stuff, not asking us. But she told us about a family she knew. The father died and the mother had two daughters to bring up but she didn't have any money, so the kids had to go to like an orphanage run by nuns, who were really cruel. They made the children wash their own pants when they were dirty and they had to learn all this religious stuff. The nuns told the kids if they didn't go to church every Sunday they would go to hell. Scary stuff, eh?

Anyway, said Hicksy, one day this boy in the school was accused of stealing a watch. The nuns got all the children into the main hall, then one of them took his trousers down and hit his bare backside with a plank of wood in front of all the other children. Sounds bloody painful, doesn't it? Hicksy said the boy was crying more from humiliation that from pain.

Funny, while she was telling us all this stuff, Hicksy's voice sounded a bit odd, like she had something stuck in her throat. Afterwards, Sheila Ashley said she could see tears in the corners of her eyes. When she finished the story Hicksy finished the lesson ten minutes early and told us to revise our assignments cos she had to dash off and do something else.

Course the swots did what the teacher told us but the rest of us just farted around. Dave and Timbo and me played poker. Sheila told us she reckoned that Hicksy was talking about herself. Maybe, we said, then we told her to bugger off so we could concentrate on the cards.

I thought about the story afterwards and wondered whether Sheila was right about Hicksy. But it's weird, isn't it. These nuns are supposed to do what Jesus says but I can't imagine Jesus walloping some poor sod with a plank of wood.

Like I told you before, I don't normally bother much about religious stuff. But what about this - in the New Bible Jesus Christ always hangs around with poor people and sick people and that. So he obviously preferred them to rich people and important people. Is that why churches are big fancy buildings with loads of coloured windows and statues? Cos obviously they must have loads of money to pay for stuff like that. You see, if they gave their money to the poor people they wouldn't be poor anymore so they wouldn't be the sort of people Jesus liked. So they spend the money on other stuff instead. It makes sense to me. So therefore the answer to Hicksy's question is 'no' - it's wrong for rich people to give their money to poor people, despite what Martin says.

'PEOPLE WOULDN'T WANT JESUS
HANGING AROUND'

Mind you, people round here wouldn't want Jesus hanging around anyway, not when he looks like a foreigner. Even if he was wearing normal clothes they wouldn't like the long hair and the beard. They'd say he was an asylum seeker or a terrorist and they'd tell him to go back to where he came from.

They never mention poverty during Choral Evensong. Mind you, a lot of the prayers and that are in church English so they may be going on about it and I don't realise. Last Wednesday was Exeter Cathedral. Some good stuff. They did a fantastic anthem I never heard before - 'The souls of the righteous are in the hands of God'. I've listened to the recording hundreds of times and I really dig it.

You know what? I played the melody to Miss Hochdorfer and she took over and played all four parts and sang the words as well. It's one of her favourites too. The ending is so cool. They sing 'but they are in peace' over and over, like a rondo, the last one pianissimo, ending with the melody on the fifth. It's wicked. I must try and get it on a CD or download it off the internet.

CHAPTER 4

Monday today, which means we have to write our diaries. Most of the other kids are too daft to realise that if you write interesting stuff Mrs Hicks reads it out in class. Of course that's what Sarah likes, but no-one can make out what she's on about cos she uses poncy words. Her Dad took her to London where he works in a bank and she was rabbitting on about the euro and the dollar. As far as I could make out the euro will only last twenty years and then it will be taken over by the world dollar. That's stupid - the euro hasn't even started yet in England. If Sarah's Dad is right why don't we start using the dollar now?

I was going to write up last Saturday's match. To be fair it wasn't one of Spurs' best games. They were losing one nil to Everton and Fernandez got sent off for thumping one of the Everton strikers. Luckily we sneaked a last minute equaliser, probably off-side but the ref let it go. Hicksy hates football - she keeps telling me to write something else so I thought I'd do something funny - like Amy getting told off for treading on ants. Me and Justin were playing on the computer. The door to the garden was open and outside we could see Amy stamping on the patio. We told her to stop cos the noise was putting us off. Then Mum came out and asked her what she was doing. Treading on ants, said Amy. Why, said Mum. Don't know, said Amy. So then Mum goes on about what about all the Mummy and Daddy ants waiting at home for the children to come back and now they won't cos Amy's killed them. So then Amy bursts into tears and runs inside to her room. Just and me burst out laughing - what a scream. Then Mum had a go at us, saying it's not funny and going on about the sankerty of life - I don't know what this means.

To be honest I can't make up my mind about the teachers reading your stuff out. They do it for the kids' diaries, like I told you, and also for essays you write. The trouble is you get the piss taken out of you if it's your stuff. Ollie's working out a league table for the children in my class. Of course Dave Bresson is at the top of the table. His work is so pants it never gets read out. Sarah Haywood is at the bottom, but you'd expect that. I'm about the middle or a bit below. You know what - I'd really like to do an essay about Choral Evensong, but you can imagine what the other boys would say. I'd get sent to the bottom of the league, even below Sarah. It's too risky - I've got to protect my image!

On Choral Evensong they even sing the prayers. It's weird - the preacher does a long prayer on one note, a bit boring, then the choir does a really fancy 'amen' in full harmony taking several bars. I got to thinking - when we used to say our prayers when I was a kid I used to pray for Mum and Dad and Granny and

Grandad Fielding and Granny Forester and Uncle Maurice and Auntie Jessica and my disgusting sisters and all my friends and that. Then I used to pray for sick people and poor people, like I was taught. But then I thought that's unfair - what about all the billions of people you leave out. What happens to them? Okay, maybe they've got their own families to pray for them but you can see it's bloody complicated. Suppose someone gets missed out? Why doesn't everyone just pray for everyone else so it all evens out? Anyway, if God was as terrific as they make out he would want to help people without being asked to. So why bother with prayers anyway?

I get these funny ideas sometimes. In school we were doing the nervous system and Mrs Hicks was telling us when you see something or hear something or touch something or smell something it's only messages from your nerves to your brain. So I suddenly thought - suppose I am the only person here in the whole universe. Everything else is just pictures and sounds in my brain. Scary, isn't it? When I told Hicksy the other kids laughed and Dave Bresson pulled my hair. 'Big shot,' he said. '*I'm* the only person in the universe, not you.' But Hicksy said I had a good point but I wasn't the first to think it. These Greek guys in the olden days talked about stuff like that, she said. There was even a name for it - she wrote it on the board - solipsism - where you think you're the only thing that exists.

Dave then said that I was the biggest areshole in the universe but unfortunately for him Hicksy heard him and gave him a bollocking. Everybody sniggered, except Sheila Ashley, who turned round to look at me with a sort of smile on her face.

'THE TEACHERS DON'T LIKE IT
OF COURSE'

I'm changing my mind about Sheila. We were all messing around in the playground during break one day and someone said 'what about a shit-shouting competition'. It's dead easy - all you've got to do is shout the word 'shit' as loud as you can and make it last as long as possible. The teachers don't like it of course so we have to check they aren't around when we do it. It's boys only, although we sometimes let Denise join in because she's really good. As usual, Dave Bresson was winning when my turn came. I took a deep breath and was just about to start when I saw Sheila watching me. It was like she wanted to say 'please don't do it'. I got confused. I thought, I'll do it really really loud just to wind her up but then for some reason I stopped and pretended to have a sudden cough. Someone else took my turn and I didn't do a shit-shout at all. I looked at Sheila again and she looked at me. I went all funny inside and could feel my face going red.

Now I find I'm trying to do things to make her like me. I've even started going to Mrs Wright's Latin class after school on Tuesday because Sheila goes and I can talk to her without my mates seeing. They still take the piss though – once for going to Latin and twice for doing it to meet Sheila. I thought it would be boring – well, it is boring – although it might help if I want to learn the words of church music – some of it is in Latin. Mrs Wrong says Latin in useful if you want to learn other languages or want to understand complicated English words. Well, that's a waste of time – everyone abroad speaks English these days and only showoffs like Sarah Haywood use big words. But at least I now know that Agnus Dei means 'Lamb of God' and Adeste Fideles means 'O Come All Ye Faithful'. Possum is not just a furry animal, but means 'I can' in Latin. Video means 'I see'.

It's because of Sheila that Dave Bresson laughed at me for answering a question from the teacher. Mrs Bellwood asked us what the word 'ambiguous' meant. Of course Sarah put her hand up but no-one else did. Funnily enough I knew the answer, but I thought if I put my hand up the other boys will kill me. But then I thought, why not annoy Sarah and show off to Sheila at the same time? Mrs Bellwood was amazed when my hand went up. Sarah looked really pissed off when Bellwood chose me. It was fantastic. I couldn't see Sheila's face because she sits in front of me. I hope she was impressed.

CHAPTER 5

Actually, it was my piano teacher, Miriam Hochdorfer, who told me what 'ambiguous' meant. Sometimes in the lesson she gives me a break and plays stuff herself. She was playing something by an American bloke called Gershwin. I said it sounded a bit like jazz and she started telling me about blue notes. That's not the colour blue, by the way. It's just that you change some of the notes on the normal scale.

If you've got a piano or a keyboard you can prove it yourself. Play a C major chord but then drop the top note to B flat so you've got a seventh. Now here's where the ambiguous bit comes in - you can play either E natural or E flat to get a blues chord. You can even play them both in the same chord. Miriam calls it the 'ambiguous third', which is how I got to know what it meant. She played some more Gershwin then suddenly stopped, but leaving her fingers on the notes.

'Look,' she said. 'B with the left hand and B flat with the right'. Those are the third notes in the G scale, if you didn't know already. She hit the notes again. It made a sort of tingly sound. Then she carried on with the piece.

She's got an old photo on the piano, black and white. There's a young girl about the same age as my sister Amy and a man and a woman about my Mum's age. I'd always thought the girl was Miriam herself, but in the photo she's holding a violin. One day not long ago she saw me looking at it and began to tell me about it.

'Yes, that was me, many years ago. And my mother and father'. In the picture Miriam and her Dad are smiling but her Mum looks sad.

'You used to play the violin, then,' I said.

'Yes.'

'Can you still play?'

'No, I have not touched a violin for over sixty years.'

Her eyes went a bit squinty and she seemed to be trying to remember something. There was a silence and I didn't know what to say. I thought, wow, what happened to suddenly make her stop?

'Didn't you like playing it then?' I asked

'At first yes, then no.'

I felt a bit, you know, embarrassed, like I could tell something was wrong.

'It's incredible what people can do to other people,' said Miriam. 'Man's inhumanity to man. Civilisation is such a thin veneer. You see, people are animals. In fact worse than animals - sometimes they are deliberately cruel.'

I started to get a bit panicky. I didn't understand what she was talking about and I thought maybe she'd gone mad. She lives on her own so there was no-one I could call to for help. I didn't know what to do.

'Shall I carry on with what I was playing?' I said, hoping that would make everything normal again.

'It was the war,' said Miriam. 'We had to leave Austria after my father was arrested.'

I decided to let her say whatever she wanted to say - get it out of her system, like. But I would have to tell Mum just in case she really was losing her marbles.

'The Gestapo took my father away one evening. I had just gone to bed when I heard the door knocker. There were voices downstairs and I heard my mother calling, "don't take him, don't take him. He has done nothing." I was very scared and I got out of bed and went to the top of the stairs. There were two men in the hall, in civilian clothes, with my parents. My mother was crying and waving her arms and my father was trying to calm her, saying it was just routine and he would be back soon. He saw me standing on the stairs and he smiled at me and blew me a kiss. "See you tomorrow, darling," he said. Then he went out with the two men. My mother stood crying at the open door, calling, "please let him come home, please, please, please . . ."'

I could picture what Miriam was talking about in my mind. I've seen war films where people get dragged off by the Germans. But this was for real.

'We never saw him again,' she said.

Miriam looked calmer now. I thought, I'm glad the story's over - I don't like sad things - but what has it got to do with the violin?

But the story wasn't over.

'My mother heard that father had been deported, probably to a concentration camp. She decided we had to get away. My younger brother Theo had already been sent to stay with friends in Torino so there was just the two of us left.'

'Why did they arrest your Dad?' I asked.

'He called a public meeting to protest about something, I can't remember what it was. Something to do with politics, probably. Although he was an architect he was also involved in politics before the war.'

'So is that how you came to England?' I said.

Miriam shook her head. 'No, we were going to Torino to join Theo. My mother locked up the house and we walked to the station. The two of us, two suitcases and my violin. My mother's flute was in one of the cases - she played in the Kanzelkehre symphony orchestra. It was winter, very cold, and the train was late but there weren't any problems until we got to Bolzano, where we had to change to another train, the one that was going to Milano and Torino.

'This train was also late. All the trains were late in the war. My mother and I went to the ladies' waiting room but there was no fire so it was freezing. It was nearly midnight. We were the only two there.

'Two German soldiers came into the waiting room. They looked young to me, not much more than boys. It was obvious they were drunk. My mother politely informed them that the room was for ladies only. One of the soldiers swore at her and told her to get out. My mother looked calm but I was scared. She said to me: "Come on, dear, we'll wait outside. The train won't be long now."

But the soldier stopped her getting to the door. "No," he said, "stay here."

"We are happy to wait outside," said my mother. "Please let us pass." I could see the other soldier smiling, but not in a nice way.

The first soldier looked at me. I was very scared. "You play the violin, little girl?"

I was too frightened to answer. He came over and stood in front of me. I could smell the drink on his breath. "I said, do you play the violin?"

My mother replied, "Yes, she does."

The soldier came closer. "I'm talking to you, little Austrian slut," he said. I could feel his spittle on my face.

"Yes," I said.

"Then play it," he said.

I looked up at Mother. Her eyes were frightened too but she smiled at me. "Would you like to play a tune for the soldier?" she said.

I could feel tears running down my face but I smiled back and said, "Yes, mother."

The soldier moved back and took a seat on the bench opposite us. "Play the Beethoven Concerto," he said. "It's one of my favourites. Play the last movement."

Again I looked at Mother. I didn't know this piece, not at that time anyway. My mother told the soldier that I couldn't play it. The soldier looked at his friend for a moment then turned to Mother. "Are you Jewish?" he asked her.

"No," said Mother.

"You look Jewish to me, both of you." He spoke to me. "Are you Jewish, little girl?"

I couldn't speak. I just shook my head.

"If you are Jewish you have to go to the Special Camp, do you understand?"

"We are not Jewish," said Mother.

"I don't believe you. But if your daughter - she is your daughter? - if she plays the Beethoven I will not tell anyone that you are trying to escape going to the Special Camp."

"May I help her, please? She can play it if I play the flute accompaniment."

The soldier looked puzzled. "What flute accompaniment?"

"You know," said my mother, "the arrangement by Vogel."

The soldier waved his hand dismissively. "Alright, I permit you."

My mother opened her suitcase and took out the flute. I got my violin out of its case. I couldn't hold it properly because my hands were shaking because I was scared and the room was cold. Mother said quietly to me: 'It's in D major, triple time, one eighty to the minute. Just repeat the phrases I play. It's quite easy."

We started to play and I tried to copy her but it was difficult to play the notes accurately. I made lots of mistakes and the more I panicked the worse I played. The soldier stood up again and motioned us to stop. I thought he was going to tell me off for playing out of tune but instead he spoke to mother.

"Your coat is hindering your playing. The arms are too heavy - you're not holding the flute correctly. Take off your coat."

"Sir, it's very cold," said Mother. "I would prefer to keep it on. I can still play properly."

"Take it off."

Mother put down her flute and took off her coat. Underneath she was wearing just a blouse. She picked up the flute again.

'HOW COULD ANYONE BE SO NASTY TO
A LADY AND A LITTLE GIRL'

"Now play."

I tried really hard to follow Mother but she was shivering and it made her play badly. Again the soldier stopped us.

"Take off your blouse," he said.

Mother pleaded with him. I could see she was close to tears. I put down the violin and threw my arms round her, trying to keep her warm.'

Miriam stopped for a moment and this time her eyes were watering. It must have been horrible in the station, being bullied by drunk soldiers. How could anyone be so nasty to a lady and a little girl?

'We heard a whistle then and a few moments later our train pulled in. I watched the carriage windows as they went by, hoping someone would see us as the train slowed down. Someone who could rescue us. There were some passengers on it but they were not paying attention. Some of them were asleep.

"Please, this is our train. Please may we go?" asked Mother. But the soldier then pulled his pistol out of its holster and pointed at us.

"Take off your blouse or I will shoot your daughter."

The carriage opposite the waiting room had a passenger sitting right by the window, a man reading the paper. The engine blew its whistle again and the man in the train put down his paper and checked his watch. He looked round and looked into the waiting room. I thought, surely he must see us, a soldier pointing a gun at two civilians. Surely he could investigate. But the soldier told his friend to pull down the window blind. So that avenue of rescue was closed.

"I'm waiting," said the soldier holding the gun.

With shaking hands my mother took my arms away and started to unbutton her blouse. I just lost control and burst into tears. I ran to the soldier, screaming, "No! No! No!" but he pushed me away.

"Get back!" he shouted.

Just then the door opened and another German soldier came in, an officer. He looked at the four of us and addressed the man with the gun.

"What's going on?" he asked.

"These two Jews have escaped custody. I have just arrested them," said the soldier.

The officer came over to us. He was not smiling and his eyes had no message.

"Madam, you look cold. Why aren't you wearing your coat?"

"I told her to take it off, sir," said the soldier behind him. "I wanted her daughter to play the Beethoven concerto and she was playing the flute accompaniment. But she couldn't play it properly because her coat was too bulky."

"Please, put on your coat," said the officer. "I must say, I didn't realise there was a part for solo flute in that piece."

"There isn't, sir, I'm sure," said the soldier. 'They were just making it up. They said it was the Vogel arrangement, but there's no such thing."

"Ah, the Vogel arrangement." The officer turned to us. "Excuse me, madam, may I see your papers?"

My mother was still putting on her coat so I got the documents out of her bag and gave them to the officer. But at that moment the engine whistled again and the train began to pull out.

"Sir, that is our train," my mother said to the officer. "We are going to Torino."

The officer nodded, still checking the documents. We couldn't see the train because the blind was down but we could hear the engine exhaust getting faster. Then the officer returned the documents and smiled briefly at us and walked out of the room. Above the noise of the train we could hear orders being shouted. Suddenly there was a screech of brakes and we could hear the train stopping. The two soldiers who had threatened us looked very sullen. I hoped they would not hurt us. My mother asked if she could pack her flute away but there was no reply, so she did it anyway. I put my violin in its case but I was still scared. The soldier with the gun still had it in his hand.

The officer came back in. "The train is waiting for you," he said. "I have instructed the conductor to look after you and make sure you get safely to Torino." He turned to the soldiers. "Go and wait for me in the Stationmaster's office. I will be along shortly."

When they had gone the officer picked up our cases, one in each hand, and we went to the train and got on, Mother carrying my violin. The officer put our cases on the luggage rack and asked us to sit down.

"I apologise for the behaviour of those two," he said. "War is not good for youngsters. It damages their hearts and their souls and they forget their manners. I will remind them that it is impolite to point guns at defenceless ladies. By the way, my son is a musician, in the Stuttgart Philharmonic. He plays the cello. I know Beethoven very well. Is there such a thing as the Vogel arrangement?"

"No," said Mother. "I was trying to help my daughter."

The officer nodded. "Well, maybe there should be. Have a good journey."

And that was it. He got off the train and waved to us from the platform as it pulled out again. The rest of the journey was uneventful. The conductor made sure we were comfortable and even brought us food and coffee. He wouldn't let Mother pay for anything - said it was all taken care of.'

'Was everything okay in Italy?' I asked.

Miriam nodded. 'Yes, we were well looked after, considering our friends had very little money and we had virtually nothing. When we arrived Mother said we'd have to sell her flute and my violin to help pay for our keep, and her best clothes too. She said we should play the instruments together before they were sold and she arranged a little concert for the Barbiere family - the friends we were staying with.'

Miriam was quiet again for a minute, obviously going back to the past.

'I took my violin out of its case while Mother tuned her flute and then - and I don't know why - I suddenly couldn't bear to touch it. I threw it onto the floor and stamped on it until it was smashed to pieces. The others were amazed. Then I realised what I'd done and I burst into tears. Mother came over and hugged me and said she understood. She wasn't angry that I'd destroyed something that could be sold to buy food. That was the last time I held a violin in my hands. I still can't, although I can listen to the D major concerto now without getting upset.'

'How did you end up in England?' I asked her.

'Just before the end of the war the Italian family had to move to England because Signor Barbiere - the head of the family - had to do work here. Mother didn't want us to stay in Torino on our own so we went to England with them. She thought it was too risky to go back to Austria until the war was over. Then after the war when the family went back to Italy the three of us stayed here while Mother made arrangements for us to go back to Austria, to Jenbach, our village. She flew to Innsbruck to find us somewhere to live. A friend had told her someone else was living in our house. My mother didn't know if she could get our house back or if she would have to find somewhere else.'

'Did you get your house back?' I asked.

Miriam shook her head. 'Mother never arrived. The plane crashed into the mountains when it was coming into land. Everyone was killed.'

I didn't say anything. Miriam picked up the photo on the piano and stared at it. She wasn't crying or anything, just staring.

'It was the middle of the night,' she said after a while. 'There was a snowstorm.'

Miriam looked at me with like a sad smile. 'Bad luck . . . good luck . . . how can you explain it?'

I didn't understand what she meant so I just shrugged.

'Bad luck . . . Father was taken away and killed by the Germans . . . good luck . . . the rest of us survived. Bad luck . . . those soldiers at Bolzano finding us . . . good luck . . . the officer letting us go. Bad luck . . . Mother getting that flight. The plane was delayed so instead of arriving in Innsbruck in daylight in good weather they arrived in the middle of the night in a snowstorm. Afterwards they said the pilot made a mistake with the navigation. Maybe he was tired.'

'So you never went back?'

Again Miriam shook her head. 'No, Theo and I both stayed in England with people my mother had made friends with. We didn't want to go back. A few years later we went to Torino for a vacation and stayed with the Barbiere family. Theo fell in love with a local girl and ended up marrying her, so eventually he went to Italy to live there. I didn't want to go to Jenbach on my own and leave my English friends so I never went back.'

'Do you ever go to see your brother?' I said.

'I used to but he died a few years ago. There's just me now.'

CHAPTER 6

Afterwards I thought what an amazing story. You look at Miriam and she's just a little old lady who plays the piano. And yet those things happened to her, just like a movie or something. I wondered if she'd ever got married or had children. It's not as if she was ugly. She was wrinkly, yes, but maybe when she was younger she looked good.

'RIGHT, FINGERS ON BUZZERS FOR YOUR
GENERAL KNOWLEDGE QUESTIONS'

And this thing about Jewish people, you still get that today. In school we learnt that the Jewish people and the Arabs have hated each other for like thousands of years. It's religion again, fighting about whose God is the best one. All these religions in the world, each one thinks it's got the best God. But how can you tell? It's not like there's a way of checking it out, like a competition or something. The Arabs also hate the Americans, because the main God in America is money and also America helps Israel, which is where the Jews live, except that lots of Jewish people live in America, which is why they help Israel. The Arabs hate the Americans so much they blew up the World Trade Centre in New York with two airliners. So then the Americans smashed up Iraq when they bombed Saddam with Weapons of Mass Distraction, which confuse the enemy by making them look the other way while you drop bombs on them. Then you've got like Catholics and Protestants hating each other in Ireland and Scotland. And blacks and whites in Africa and blacks and whites and Asians here in England.

Hicksy asked us how you could stop people hating each other. Sarah came out with some big words but what she meant was - I think - babies don't hate other babies when they're born - it's grown-ups who teach them how to hate. My idea was - if people have been taught to hate other people, why couldn't they be taught to de-hate them? Hicksy said good thinking you two, which of course was very embarrassing for me, although Sarah loved it. Sheila Ashley was off sick so I didn't even get a smile from her. I told the grown-ups about it when I went round to Justin's after school and Martin said he would put it in his speech. I said okay, but for Christ's sake don't say my name! Justin's Dad's girlfriend told me off for blasphemy, which is when you say bad things about Jesus and that, but that's stupid - how can a dead person living in another country hear what you're saying?

Martin says the Jews and the Arabs will soon be fighting over water, not religion, because of global warming. I must say, ever since people started going on about global warming the weather seems to be getting colder in England. And more rain as well. But apparently in the place where the Arabs and the Jews are the water is getting less. But then people say the sea level will go up, which is more water, not less. Why can't they use this water if there's not enough?

But you can get good things out of global warming, like cars automatically washing themselves. You see, every car in the world makes about four thousand kilos of carbon dioxide every year - that's like four tonnes. Think how many billions of cars there are in the world and you can see how much of this stuff gets into the atmosphere. Well, carbon dioxide traps the sun's heat which means more water evaporates from the sea, which means more clouds and more rain, which washes the cars! Except where the Jews and Arabs live - they would still have to use the car wash.

'... CARS AUTOMATICALLY WASHING
THEMSELVES ...'

Mrs Hicks set us an essay for homework. Are cars good or bad? I wrote down that everyone says there should be less cars but no-one wants to give theirs up. There was a programme on the telly the other day about what people do with their cars. How about this - they showed a gym where people get on a walking machine, you know the thing, like a moving rubber belt which you walk on but you stay in the same place. But people drive to the gym to do walking exercise! Is that weird, or what? Why don't they just walk to the gym in the first place if they want to practise walking? Guess what the answer would be if you asked them! They also showed a clip from

America where a woman came out of a shop, got into her car, then drove about 50 metres to another shop and got out again! We were allowed to ask our parents and friends for ideas for the essay. As you know, Martin's always going on about cars and things. When he's in his own car he says it annoys him when he lets people cross the road on pedestrian crossings but they never say thankyou. He said they were very rude. But he wants to help pedestrians who aren't rude – he doesn't like people driving in the evening or in bad weather with only their parking lights on. He says he would make a law saying people would have to use their headlights so pedestrians can see them better. Mum said she turns her mirror pointing down so she can't see people driving too close behind her – she says it scares her. My Dad said Mum was silly to do that and he also said that most people in the world drive their cars on the wrong side of the road. In my essay I put that I want a car when I grow up but I want it to use fuel that doesn't harm the world.

You've probably had enough of all this crap I've been telling you so I'll pack it in now. If you're not completely bored, you can read a copy of Martin's speech. You can see the ideas he got from me. Most of the rest is a load of rubbish, going on about education and politics and stuff – ignore those bits if you want. There's a bit about a train crash as well, where the driver was going too fast and the train came off the rails, which sounds a dozy kind of thing to do but Martin told me . . . it's not as simple as that!

Actually Charlie did a lot of work on the speech. Did I tell you she's a journalist, which as you know is someone who gets ideas from other people and writes about it in the papers. That's why the stuff they write is called 'copy'. She's dead clever, Charlie. She knows the meaning of every word in the English language. Just to test her, I asked her what 'solipsism' meant and she knew the answer straight away. I asked her why she didn't write stories to make more money. She told me she'd written three whole books but no-one would make copies for the bookshops. There are people called publishers who are supposed to do this but it's difficult to make them print your story. Martin says there's a special problem that causes it, called Catch-22. This means that you can't get your book published till you've already had other books published. If that's true then maybe Charlie isn't that clever after all - she's never had a book published so she's never going to make it so she's wasting her time writing books in the first place.

CHAPTER 7

Let me start by introducing myself. For those of you who don't know me, I am a senior driver with South Midland, based at High Wycombe. I've been with South Mid since before privatisation. Like most of the private companies we've had our troubles and our customers still refer to us as the Sado-Masochists.

The good news is that the the directors are finally coming to realise that a well-trained, motivated, properly-rewarded workforce actually improves the efficiency of the railway business. It's a pity it's taken them so long to discover what a child of eight could tell you - if you treat people well they will work better for you than if you bully them. And it's pleasing to see some of the ancient rolling stock finally being carted off to the breakers' yard. But we can only give the directors two cheers. The modernisation and new investment is still too slow. This country's railway system is a good example of the old saying that the British way is 'muddling through with inadequate resources.' And bad operational practices are still lurking in many areas of the industry. The Aylesbury incident which some of you are familiar with is a case in point and I shall be referring to it again later in this speech.

I have two areas of concern in the activities of our Union. Firstly, most of you will know that I am Vice-Chairman of the Working Practices Committee and that I also serve on the Train Operating Companies' Arbitration Board. This work takes up about two thirds of my Union time. The rest of it is spent on Developing World problems. I'm proud to say that we're in the forefront of British Trades Union activity in this area and I'm proud to be Chairman of the Developing World Aid Committee.

I am standing for re-election to the National Executive so that I can continue my work on the committees I serve on. I have been involved with industrial relations work for the Union for nearly twenty years, although there were times in the immediate post-privatisation period when I seriously thought of chucking in the towel. I don't think I was alone in that respect. In fact I will confess to you that I was so demoralised I even considered leaving the industry. It was my partner, Charlotte, who talked me round, or should I say bullied my into facing up to my responsibilities. It was Charlotte who pointed out that when people are demoralised they need someone to rally them to fight back and she virtually ordered me to pick myself up and get on with it.

She's in the building somewhere as an observer, so let me say publicly - Thank you, Charlie - for firing me up. She'll probably tell me off afterwards for mentioning it.

I have to confess she helped me write this speech - she's a journalist and her English is better than mine - but she didn't know I was going to mention her name.

I said before that the Developing World is an important part of our union activity. We're doing a lot in this area but I'd like to see us do more. We've been through difficult times in this industry and maybe we've been so wrapped up in our own troubles that we've forgotten about people less fortunate than ourselves. We really ought to be ashamed at how the rich nations are so unwilling to share their wealth with the poor ones.

Thankfully the worst excesses of monetarism that swept through the Developed World in the 80s and 90s are now behind us and at last there are signs that people are being valued more than money, in some industrial enterprises at least. What our union and similar organisations need to do now is increase that momentum. We have to educate our children that it is not acceptable to think only of themselves - they must be taught that they will have to do their bit to help people who by sheer bad luck are born into poverty or ignorance.

Because that's what it comes down to - luck. Take a look at me - I've been very lucky. I was born to loving parents who weren't rich but they weren't poor either. I got a decent education at the expense of the state. I have no disabilities and I have white skin. Suppose I'd been born disabled, or a black in one of our inner cities. What sort of life would I have had? With loving, supportive parents I might have had a chance to do well. But suppose I was the child of a single parent who was too exhausted by life to look after me properly and went to a school with no resources, where the teachers were demoralised and academic expectation was zero. Would it be so surprising if I went outside the law to get things that I would otherwise have no chance of getting? Would it be so surprising if I resorted to drugs or alcohol to bring relief from the unremitting misery of life? What would people expect me to **do** with my life?

Now imagine that problem times ten. Imagine being born in a poor African or Asian country. What would you have to look forward to in life? Not enough food, no money, no education, no work, or even worse - slavery, nowhere decent to live. Nothing. What sort of life is that? Suppose someone came along and said, 'Join my organisation and I'll make it better for you. Help me fight the infidels who steal our resources and starve us.' Would you be able to resist? Perhaps poverty and exploitation are two of the the seeds of terrorism.

And now here's the really big question. Should the lucky people be expected to help the unlucky ones? There are plenty of people who will tell you 'no', but you won't find them in Bangladesh or Nicaragua or Somalia. You'll find them in financial centres in London and New York and Frankfurt and Paris. You'll find them in big comfortable houses and big comfortable cars. If you say to them, 'why don't you want to share your good luck?' they'll say why should they? They'll tell you they worked hard to get their money. Some of them even pay their taxes. They'll conveniently forget that they were lucky to be born with the talent for making money and they won't mention the workers they exploited to get that money.

'IMAGINE ALL THE PEOPLE SHARING
ALL THE WORLD'

What we have to do is change the minds of these people - not the older ones - they're a lost cause. It's back to education - social education if you like. We must teach gifted and talented children to share the fruits of their good luck. They should be guided by the words of John Lennon: 'Imagine all the people sharing all the world'.

It might surprise some of you to hear me say that socialism is not the answer - not in the old-fashioned sense of the word. The idea of 'from each according to his ability, to each according to his needs' was bound to be a failure, because it ignores human nature. I'll use myself as an example again. The most important people to me are me and Charlotte, then my brother and my parents, then other members of my family, then friends and so on.

Selfishness is a natural human characteristic. So what we have to say to our children is - look, you've got ability and talent - use those abilities and talents to do well for yourself, to get a good job, make a good living, nice house, nice car etc. You don't need to feel guilty about earning wealth but while you're doing it, spare a thought for the unlucky ones, born without talent or ability or into poverty.

Actually, sparing a thought is not enough. Nor even is giving money to charity, although that helps of course. No, we must say to the next generation, your social duty is to give time and effort to improve the lot of the unlucky ones. Remember, we must tell our children, every person who is born into this world is entitled to expect freedom from hunger, basic education, health care, work to do, and most important of all, some happiness in their lives and a sense of purpose. It's up to the lucky ones to make sure the unlucky ones get these basic human rights.

Some entrepreneurs will tell you they're already helping the third world by setting up industries there. But of course they're not really helping the local people, they're helping themselves. Ruthless competition, one of the nastier aspects of monetarism, has forced companies to relocate to parts of the world where labour is cheap and yet again it's the the unlucky ones - many of them children - who lose out.

We need to see the process work in reverse, by setting global trade rules which prevent exploitation of workers. I'm talking about minimum wages and maximum working hours. Competition itself is no bad thing and helps to increase efficiency, but that efficiency must not be at the expense of the weakest people. Rather, there must be basic rights for workers everywhere in the world and efficiency achieved through the way businesses are managed rather than by abuse of the workforce. And, as I've previously mentioned, by removing the seething resentment fuelled by grinding poverty and exploitation you'll reduce terrorism too. You cannot make a terrorist out of a contented person.

Again, forget the present day entrepreneurs and company directors. Their education was flawed - they weren't taught their social duty. They were brought up to worship the great god, money. No, the children of today are the ones who need to learn these new responsibilities. And in turn they will pass the message on to their children and then the world may see a fairer disribution of wealth and power. My girlfriend, Charlotte, who's better educated than me, has supplied a quote from the poet Wordsworth, who said in eight words what I've been rambling on about these last ten minutes - the child is the father of the man. In other words - bring the children up right and they'll turn into good citizens and good parents.

Let us be the first generation of whom our successors can say - they taught their children correctly. Wouldn't we prefer that than if they said - they were the ones who abused the world's resources, who poisoned the oceans and polluted the atmosphere, who allowed corrupt politicians to lie their way out of trouble, who thought profit was more important than people, who thought image was more important than truth.

Let's look at that last point a bit closer. Today more than ever before we are influenced by image presenters. They are so clever they can actually change what seems to be the truth, often by the simple technique of choosing the right name. Sometimes their job is made easier because people don't want to hear the truth. It's not a new phenomenon - several hundred years ago a religious group invented the Inquisition, an innocuous name which hid the practice of torture and murder they were using to enforce political control, much the same as the concept of Rehabilitation in Stalin's Russia and Mao's China.

Today, George Orwell's character Winston Smith would be cynically amused to note that when the nuclear power station at Winscale in Cumbria ran into an image problem over radiation contamination the problem was solved by changing its name to Sellafield. In the Eighties the Poll Tax was called the Community Charge and then - a rare example of truth almost breaking out - became the Council tax. A wry smile would perhaps cross Winston Smith's lips when he heard about the worldwide practice of politicians and officials being paid bribes - sorry, I used the wrong word there - I meant to say consultation fees - by commercial enterprises trying to get what they want. And what about Genetically Modified crops now turning into Genetically Enhanced crops? Can we believe the agro-chemical companies who tell us there are no ill effects? I read in a paper recently that some biologists think it'll be decades before evidence of harm arises, by which time it might be too late to repair. Why are we rushing into it? You know the answer - to make money.

Another everyday example if misleading language you'll all be familiar with. You've phoned up a shop or a business and you're trying to talk to a real human being. You've been pressing button this and button that to navigate yourself through an interminable menu. You know what you'll hear at the end of this odyssey – tinny pop music punctuated with pre-recorded statements such as 'all our operatives are busy' or 'we are currently experiencing heavy demand'. These are euphemsims for 'we don't employ sufficient staff to deal with incoming phone calls because cutting back on personnel enables us to pay even more in obscene bonuses to the directors who did the cutting back.' To add insult to injury you may be asked to keep holding on by lies such as 'your call is important to us.' Oops – I made a mistake there. Did you notice it? I said 'personnel' when I should have said 'human resources'.

The Winston Smith character in the book 1984 thought that the only hope of changing things for the better lay with the proletariat. I humbly disagree. I think that hope lies with the children, as long as we teach them how to turn the world into a better place, with the lucky ones helping the unlucky ones, and everyone acknowledging their social responsibilities and their duty of care to planet Earth. A young lad who lives

74

near me suggested that we should teach people not to hate each other but to de-hate each other. I like that word - it could catch on. When you take away hate you begin to solve many of the world's problems. When you then start thinking about the welfare of those less fortunate than yourself you go further along the same road.

I'll take that idea and direct it to my other area of concern - industrial relations. I'm pleased to say we are beginning to make progress here, at least in South-Midland Rail, and, I understand, in other train operating companies too. The past tendency of directors and managers to intimidate and even bully the workforce is starting to reverse. At last they're beginning to think about the welfare of the workers and not just the bottom line on the account sheet. But there are still problems in the way humans deal with other humans in the workplace and one contentious area which is particularly significant in the public transport industry is the regulation of duty periods.

As some of you know, considerable research is being done by psychologists into how outside factors influence people's performance at work. Indeed, our union is directly involved in such a study taking place at Cambridge University. What is clear already is that although the performance of the human brain is fairly easy to measure, the ability to predict variations in performance is much more difficult. From this it follows that the current rules concerning duty periods are far too simplistic. This is where I'll bring in the Aylesbury incident I mentioned earlier.

After the horrors of recent fatal train crashes, the accident at Aylesbury did not attract such media attention. For a start, no one was killed, although there were several injuries, one or two serious. As a historical footnote, this accident was the first to be investigated under the auspices of the new Public Transport Inspectorate, set up by the government when it was finally accepted by the politicians that safety regulation could not be left in the hands of organisations who needed to turn a profit from revenues taken from the operating companies. The PTI is also responsible for the safety of air, sea and bus travel.

Let's look at Aylesbury. The sequence is quite straighforward. I'll read you the first few paragraphs of the interim report:

The train went over points at a recorded speed of 68 miles per hour, well in excess of the max permitted, which was 20. The usual track was undergoing engineering attention and the train was crossing onto an adjacent track. The restricted speed was clearly posted on the approach to the points and the lights illuminating this sign were found to be in working order. Rescue personnel who attended the scene of the crash confirmed that the lights were on and the sign was clearly visible.

The weather was poor at the time of the accident. It was still dark with heavy rain and strong winds. The leading car's windscreen wipers were found to be in good mechanical order and the wiper blades were in good condition. The driver stated that the wipers were in use when the accident occurred.

The train comprised a single four-car multiple unit. After crossing the points the lead and second cars both toppled off the track onto their left sides. The coupling broke between the second and third cars and cars three and four remained upright, although the leading bogie of the third car was derailed. Although there was spillage of diesel fuel from a ruptured tank there was no fire.

The driver and seven passengers were injured. Two of the injured passengers required hospitalisation for several days.

The train was a type SMR38 diesel-electric unit built five years ago, incorporating the Train Protection Warning System but not Automatic Train Protection. Neither of these systems would have prevented this accident as the train was proceeding under clear signals on its correct route.

The driver could not explain why he had ignored the speed limit. In questioning afterwards he stated that he could not remember observing the sign and could not say whether it was illuminated or not. He admitted that before commencing this duty he had omitted to read the current standing orders, which included the notice concerning engineering work at Aylesbury which detailed track changes and speed restrictions. However, the driver had read these notices the previous day and had in fact already driven over the affected route several times. On the day of the accident his manager had noticed that the driver seemed 'not quite with it' when he reported for duty (at 0530) and queried whether he was alright. The driver said he was. This duty was the fourth consecutive early start for this driver, but he stated afterwards that he was adequately rested and not suffering from fatigue as far as he was aware.

There was a minor technical problem with the train's alternate braking system, but inside MTS regulations. (MTS stands for minimum technical status, for those of you unfamiliar with this term. This specifies which equipment must be serviceable and which is permitted to be unserviceable).

The driver's past operational record was satisfactory. He had one Signal Passed at Danger (SPAD) incident on his record several years previously. His sickness rate was about 70% of the average. He was 38 years old.

The driver stated that there were no major worries in his domestic life at the time of the accident.

Let's ask ourselves - why did this accident happen? But first I'll answer the question that probably few of you thought to ask. How is the driver? And how are the injured passengers? My researchers found out that all seven passengers have recovered from their physical injuries, although one lady will have to use a walking stick for a while. Three of them are receiving counselling or cognitive therapy to help them overcome their fear of train travel. The driver is still off roster. He has recovered from his injuries but he has a problem with returning to driving. Despite counselling, he does not feel confident enough to resume driving and still feels gulity about the accident, both quite normal reactions according to the psychiatrists. He is not shirking work - in fact he is doing office duties which means his take-home pay is quite a bit less than when he was driving. I'm pleased to report that our union is making up most of the difference.

So, why did this driver exceed the speed limit? Let's look at some possible explanations. Did he do it deliberately, trying to crash the train? No - that would be the act of a deranged mind, and there was no evidence to support this supposition. Was it carelessness? A more likely explanation, but this man's operational history showed a conscientious, professional approach to his duties. The only blot on his copybook - a SPAD incident - occurred several years earlier. On that occasion he acknowledged his error but said that his attention might have been wandering because he had just found out his father was terminally ill. Maybe in a more enlightened future a worker in these circumstances will be encouraged to ask for relief from duty without feeling guilty or worrying about loss of income.

What about the fact that he hadn't read the operational notices that morning? Certainly an error, but more likely a lapse of memory rather than carelessness, given his background. I'll bet there isn't a driver here today who has never forgotten to read standing orders - I know I have, on more than one occasion.

What about other possibilities? Incompetence? Well, again, this driver had a good record. His performance assessments during route checks were always satisfactory or better. How about incapacitation? The evidence says no, the driver was not physically or mentally ill at the time of the accident and was in possession of all his faculties.

So we are left with a conundrum. Why did an experienced, competent, conscientious driver in good mental and physical health ignore speed restriction warnings and take his train at high speed over points which were severely speed limited?

Maybe the clues can be found in what I've just been telling you. Let me recap some of the points buried in the overall report.

Firstly, the Operations Manager at High Wycombe, where the driver's duty originated, said that the driver had seemed 'not quite with it' when he reported for work. As an aside here - the report doesn't pursue this further, but at the enquiry hearings the driver stated that the manager had asked him if he was feeling okay for duty. So, well done, manager. There are still a few around in the South-Mid who show no consideration whatsoever for the welfare of the workers they are in charge of. We need to get rid of these dinosaurs as soon as possible.

'Not quite with it.' What does that mean? I've got no training in psychology but I think I know what they're talking about. You know the feeling, we've all been there. You find yourself making more mistakes than usual and it seems that your mind is drifting when it should be concentrating on things and concentration itself is difficult. Sometimes it's after a long duty or when you get up after a sleepless night. Sometimes it's because you're not fully fit and sometimes . . . there's no apparent reason at all.

But perhaps in this case there is a reason. Let's revisit another sentence in the report. 'This duty was the fourth consecutive early start for this driver, although

81

he stated afterwards that he was adequately rested and not suffering from fatigue as far as he was aware.'

There are two big problems with fatigue. One is legal and one is physiological. If you look in the Train Operators' Procedures Manual you will find the following:

'A person shall not undertake driving duty if he knows or suspects that he may suffer the effects of fatigue during the course of that duty.'

This is one of the most controversial rules in the book. During the dark days just after privatisation many of you will have heard of drivers threatened with dismissal by their managers when they reported unfit for duty through fatigue. Some took to reporting sick when they were just over-tired, but again the new breed of hard-nosed managers started getting tough on those drivers with sickness rates higher than average. Needless to say, most of the cases were genuine and only a few were malingerers. But in the climate of fear, reported fatigue cases reduced even as productivity increased. It was a pity the public were never aware of how many of their trains were being driven by men and women whose judgement was impaired by fatigue.

Thankfully the climate is improving in this area. But there is still the remaining problem - how can a driver blame fatigue if he is involved in an incident? The legal bods will say - you've broken the law by driving when fatigued. So what will drivers say? Let me remind you again what the Aylesbury driver said: He was not suffering from fatigue **as far as he was aware.** What else could he say without being accused of breaking the rules?

As I mentioned above, there is another consequence of fatigue and that is that it impairs judgement. This means that a person suffering from fatigue might not even realise it. They may not realise that they are not in a fit state to do driving duties. Having eliminated other possible causes, my guess, although there is no proof, is that the Aylesbury driver was suffering from some form of fatigue, perhaps caused by having to report for work before 6 o'clock on four consecutive mornings.

I read somewhere recently that machines are now more reliable than humans. If this is true then the weak link in transport safety is the human being. Machines can be improved almost to the point of infallibility, but humans have taken millions of years to evolve into their current form and they still have minds and bodies naturally suited to pre-industrial life. The only safe way of allowing humans to operate complex machinery is to develop operating strategies that minimise the impact of human error when it occurs, as occur it must, and that remove the blame culture still prevalent in some industries and some countries.

This means that the whole area of human performance and variation in performance needs more research so that we can replace the current bad rules with something better, especially in the areas of maximum permitted duty periods, minimum rest periods and inhumane roster patterns. Which is where our research project at Cambridge fits in. Again, a bit of good news - the practice of rostering four consecutive earlies has now been discontinued. It took a fair amount of pressure from the union to achieve it but finally the directors agreed, maybe because they didn't want another Aylesbury - or worse. It's a small step, but a step in the right direction. Perhaps someone reminded them that the two worst disasters in the history of this country's railways both occurred early in the morning. In the first, almost a century ago, incorrect procedures were carried out by signalmen during a shift change at a signal box, partly through negligence, it has to be said. The result was a three train pile-up. In the second, half a century ago, the crew of an overnight express ran through red signals and collided with a stationary commuter train boarding passengers at a station. Again a third train hit the wreckage of the first two. In this case fog was a contributory factor. The combined death toll in these accidents was over 300, exacerbated in the first case by smashed wooden carriage bodies being set on fire by the ruptured gas lighting system, ignited by burning coals from the steam locomotives. We've made technical progress in so far as carriages are these days made of steel and lit electrically and operations in fog are much safer. But the weak link – the human being – is still not error proof.

Perhaps in the future they will be able to genetically modify - I'm sorry, I mean enhance - human beings so that they can work harder for longer without getting fatigued and without making mistakes, but that's an issue for future generations to address.

You can see that there's a link between the two themes of this speech, and that is how people treat other people. Firstly, how we, the fortunates, treat the unfortunates, and secondly, how we, the fortunates, treat each other. My view is that I would like to see Britain following a more European code of social behaviour. By this I mean the countries disparaged by some right-wing Americans as 'old Europe'. In these countries, the harshness of capitalism is tempered by the citizens' obligation of social provision for the less fortunate. It's the 'make money for yourself but don't forget about others' idea I mentioned earlier, and it's far superior to the American 'make money for yourself and don't bother about anyone else'. That's an oversimplification, of course. Many Americans show concern for others, and there is a tradition of philanthropism in the US in which those who have amassed fortunes redistribute some of it in charitable foundations and the like. But there is a difference in basic philosophy which was clearly exposed in the devastation wreaked on New Orleans by hurricane Katrina, which the fortunates escaped and the unfortunates did not. At the risk of oversimplification again, the American way could be summarised as 'money before people' and the European way 'people before money'.

In Britain over the last quarter of a century we have drifted towards the American model. For many people – the clever, talented ones – that means greater material wealth. But for many others it means the opposite. The much vaunted 'freedom of opportunity' is about as as achievable as a flight to Mars for deprived, undereducated families living in squalor in sink estates. I would be saddened to see the governments of enlightened European countries following Britain along this uncaring path in their obsession with economic competitiveness. You can predict the response of a sink estate inhabitant when he or she was informed that the country in which they lived was the world's fourth largest economy – 'What do they do with the money?'

It's a good question – what do we do with the money? Well, we spent a lot of it on the Iraq war, against the wishes of many citizens whose tax money it was. Some people will tell you that we waste money which the country can't afford on asylum seekers and illegal immigrants. You read it in some of the more rabidly xenophobic newspapers. You know the sort of thing – 'the reason we've got no NHS dentists is because the money that would pay for the dental service is being paid out instead in benefits to asylum seekers and illegal immigrants.' It's a lie of course and it deflects attention away from mis-spending of tax revenue by incompetent government. But wastage of taxpayers' money has been a complaint of the populace ever since taxes were first raised, often with some justification. I would contend that a welfare state that protects the unfortunates, even though it is also abused by benefit fraudsters, is better than no welfare state.

I was recently involved in a radio programme comparing industrial relations in Britain with those in other countries. I mentioned the anomaly that although Britons work longer hours that their continental cousins their productivity was often lower. It's not rocket science – if people are forced to carry on working when they're knackered the quality of work will suffer. In safety-critical industries such as public transport, there could be serious consequences. I mentioned the possibility of driver fatigue as a factor in the Aylesbury accident.

I also pointed out that Europeans tend to run their railways as public services rather than commercial businesses, with subsidised fares to encourage their use instead of cars. I have to tell you that at this point in the programme I was interrupted by a member of the audience, who shouted: 'Why don't you go and live abroad then if you think it's so much better?' The rest of the audience responded with a mixture of applause and jeers – it was difficult to say which was greater. When the hubbub died down I said that I was born in England and I loved England, but I wish England could be a bit more civilised. I think the applause for that comment just about beat the jeers.

Well, I can see some of you yawning, which tells me it's time to shut up before you start jeering me yourselves. So my closing words are: please give me your vote so I can continue my work in these fields.

Thank you.